A Slip of a Girl

PATRICIA REILLY GIFF

HOLIDAY HOUSE  NEW YORK

The following images are reproduced courtesy of the National Library of Ireland:
L_CAB_04918, p. 4; L_ROY_08496, p. 30; L_IMP_1507, p. 41; CLON618, p. 56;
CLON1646, p. 77; L_CAB_09217, p. 81; CLON2156, p. 97; L_ROY_01767, p. 109;
L_ROY_02921, p. 126; M56/43, p. 145; L_ROY_09179, p. 156; EPH E124, p. 178;
L_ROY_05267, p. 184; L_ROY_05256, p. 192; L_ROY_01772, p. 199;
L_IMP_1506, p. 210; L_ROY_11600, p. 232.

The photographs on the following pages are reproduced courtesy of
Historical Picture Archives:
p. 46; p. 89; p. 228.

The books referred to on page 52 are the Longford writer Maria Edgeworth's
Castle Rackrent and Jonathan Swift's *Gulliver's Travels*.

✣

HOLIDAY HOUSE is registered in the U.S. Patent and Trademark Office.
Printed and bound in June 2019 at Maple Press, York, PA, USA.
www.holidayhouse.com

First Edition
1 3 5 7 9 10 8 6 4 2

Library of Congress Cataloging-in-Publication Data

Names: Giff, Patricia Reilly, author.
Title: A slip of a girl / by Patricia Reilly Giff.
Description: First edition. | New York : Holiday House, [2019] | Summary:
"Set during the Irish Land Wars (1879–1882) this novel in verse follows
Anna Mallon through a series of tragedies as her mother dies,
older siblings immigrate to America, and she and her father and sister with
special needs are about to be evicted from their farm"—Provided by publisher.
Identifiers: LCCN 2018040274 | ISBN 9780823439553 (hardcover)
Subjects: LCSH: Ireland—History—1837–1901—Juvenile fiction.
CYAC: Novels in verse. | Ireland—History—1837–1901—Fiction.
Family life—Ireland—Fiction.
Classification: LCC PZ7.5.G54 Sl 2019 | DDC [Fic]—dc23
LC record available at https://lccn.loc.gov/2018040274

For my Longford great-grandmothers:
Elizabeth McClellan Reilly
of Clonbroney,
who survived the Hunger,
and
Anna Rogers Mollaghan,
and for her father,
Thomas of Drumlish,
who lived through the Land War,
with deepest admiration,
and for
their grandson,
William Reilly,
my dad,
with love

Home

Sounds

In the back field,
I'm bent double, hidden,
pulling up chickweed
for our tea.

Since the Ryans were tossed out,
this field belongs to the English earl,
and his sheep,
who huddle near the stone wall.

Nearby, screams begin.
They come from a mud house
that shelters a family of girls:
Bridey, Mair, Kate,
and Mag,
I forgot the new baby's name,
Cassie?

I stand tiptoed,
trying to see.

The crash comes
over their screams.
The bashing in!
Dust rises up:
the house of five girls
and a mam is gone.
They're forced out on the road,
maybe to starve.

I clutch my fist to my chest.
I'm afraid for the five girls
and the mam.
I'm afraid for us,
Mam and Da,
Willie and John,
Jane and Nuala,
and even more afraid
for me, Anna.

But didn't Da say
we're all right?

A house that has been destroyed by a battering ram during an eviction in County Clare
(This image is reproduced courtesy of the National Library of Ireland L_CAB_04918.)

The Hill

AFTER supper that night,
I climb my hill.
It's steep and rocky,
but my bare feet know the way.

I sing one of Da's old songs.
I won't think about those poor things
on the road.

From behind the hedgerow,
my brother Will says,
"She has a mouth on her,
that Anna."
And John: "With a voice like a frog."

I make a frog sound,
laughing,
and go on.
I carry an old potato,
green with mold.

If one of the little people
comes up from the earth,
I'll throw it to him,
and dash away while he eats.

From here, I can see the world,
my world anyway:
the bogs that cover the earth
like blankets,
and the snipes that fly high.
There's the top of Liam's roof,
the thatch tan with weeds.
Beyond that, the schoolhouse.
I close my eyes.
I've never been inside.
I'm needed at home.

The corn mill rises up below,
its great wheel creaking
as it grinds the grain.

The English earl's house spreads out
like a castle.
He's a man to be feared.

He could put us out to starve,
if he wished.

A sudden wind loosens a stone.
It rolls and moves another.
Something is underneath.
I catch my breath.
A book!
I've never seen one before,
except in church.

One cover is missing.
The other is the color
of a January field.
It has a picture of a horse,
its mane flying.

I clutch the book to myself,
wondering at those silky pages.
Imagine knowing what the writing says!

I fly down the hill,
to tell my best friend, Liam.
I pass my house
and circle around the Donnellys'.

The oldest, Mae, raises her hand
to wave.
She looks tired.
She has more to do than any of us,
with her da gone,
and five children in
steps and stairs
behind her.

Liam meets me
at the crumbling stone wall.
I don't say a word,
but hold the book in front of me.

"Oh, Anna," he says.
He reaches out,
almost touching it,
and then my hand.
"If only I could read," I say.
He nods.

A Word

THAT night while everyone sleeps,
I sit on the rush chair
at the hearth.
The room is cozy.
The banked glow of peat
gives enough light
to see my treasure,
the book!

I stare at the cover,
and picture the horse
pawing the ground,
as I climb on his back.
We soar across the field
and jump over the wall.

I lean closer to the firelight.
The circles and lines
under the picture must say
Horse!

A joy like listening
to Da's stories,
or swinging along the boreen
with Liam,
fills my chest
and spills into my throat.

I go to Mam's bed.
She never sleeps.
How thin she looks!
Her eyes are sunken,
her cheeks flushed.
Please, let her just be tired.

I put my hand on her shoulder.
"I can read a word."
She touches my cheek.
"Alannah, my Anna,"
she whispers.

Liam

WE sit on the stone wall,
our heads close,
and search through the book
to see *Horse*.
It's printed on almost
every page.
We know dozens of words,
all *Horse*.
But still...

"Anna?" Liam begins.
I glance at his blue-gray eyes,
the color of a windy sky.
"We haven't paid the rent,"
he says.
"Not this quarter,
not the last two."

"This year may be different,"
I say desperately.

grasping his arm.
"It's almost time to plant."

"If the weather holds,
we'll have vegetables
to sell,
and lumper potatoes to fill us
next winter."

"It's too late," Liam says,
his hand on mine.
"We'll be out on the road,
Mam and me."

I can't see the earl's house
from here.
Still I look toward it.
Rage rises up in my throat.
I swallow,
try to speak over it.
"Our land," is all I can manage.
"Someday," Liam says,
touching the curl of my hair.

Spring

MARCH is here,
time to plant.
With knives in our hands,
we cut the eyes
from seed potatoes.

We'll tuck them in the earth,
where they'll send up green shoots
and purple blossoms.
Then underneath,
lumpers!
My sister Jane is old enough
to help.
But her mind is far away,
on a ship to America.
She slices her finger
as well as the potato.

Ah, Jane.
Mam and I rub her arms,

while Willie pats her head,
and John finds a cobweb
to stop the bleeding.
Da croons, "Don't cry, *astore*."

We set the cuts in the field.
Mam bends,
trying to catch her breath,
her fine hair blowing in the breeze.
She pats the soil
the way she pats us.
"Our mother, the earth,"
she says.

Nuala grabs my skirt,
wanting a bit of potato,
not to plant, but to eat.
Her smiling face looks
almost like Mam's.
I gather her up,
twirl her around.
"Someday," I say.

If only the days are clear,
and the lumpers can grow.

"Listen, sky," I yell,
my fist raised.
"Hold back the rain
for us,
and for Liam and his mam."

Leaving

AFTER the potatoes, the oats,
and the summer cabbage
begin to grow,
Will and John go down the road,
arms slung around each other's
shoulders.

They've worked hard in town,
mucking out the hotel barn,
washing windows,
and sweeping the street.
They have enough coins now,
just,
to pay for passage.
Their ship will sail from Cork,
to Brooklyn, America.

Da stands in the field,
one hand raised in blessing.
Mam's face is set

so they won't see her tears.
I look hard after my brothers.
I'll never see them again.

"Take me," Jane cries,
until the road turns
and they're gone forever:
Willie who carried me on his shoulder
when I was Nuala's age,
and John so tough
he could walk through nettles,
but was soft for Jane.

I pick up a clod of damp earth
and hold it tight in my fist.
America is not for me.
That faraway place is for my brothers,
and maybe for Jane.
But I belong to this country.
If only it belonged to me.

Mam

IT'S early, still dark.
Mam is at the hearth.
I go to help with the cooking.

She stands, stirring,
one hand
against the stones,
balancing herself.

The wooden spoon falls
to the floor,
spattering hot soup.
She sinks down for it,
her hand sliding,
and kneels there.

I stare at her.
She's bone thin,
her hair was red
like mine

but streaked white now.
Are we going to lose her?

She turns.
I can't hide my fear.
"I'm all right, child."
She raises her shoulder
a bit.

I go toward her,
stumbling.
"I can't do without you,"
I say fiercely.
I bury my head
in her chest.
All right, I tell myself.
She's all right.

Hens

A clap of thunder,
and sudden downpour.
I open the half door,
worried about the crop.

The hens, wings flapping,
flutter along the boreen.
What's happened?

I throw my shawl
over my shoulders.
Head bent against the rain,
I run to turn them back.

But ahead of me,
arms out, reaching,
a man chases after them.
Our hens!

I'm desperate to catch them,
but I trip,

turning my ankle,
losing moments.

I scramble up.
One hen is under his arm.
He reaches for the neck
of another.
I yell,
Can anyone hear me?

But then,
Mae Donnelly stands
in front of him,
arm raised,
pitchfork over her head.

The man drops the hen,
and runs away
across the Donnellys' field.

Mae stabs the earth
with the pitchfork,
and reaches for me,
"Are you all right, Anna?"

"The hens," I say.
"How can I thank you?"

She helps me
turn them toward home,
then waves.
"We have to take care
of each other,"
she calls after me.

Last Day

EVERY day,
Mam weakens.
Then, one morning,
I kneel at the side of her bed.
"Keep Nuala safe,"
she whispers.
"The house and the land."

For a moment,
Da rests his head against hers.
"Anna's only a slip of a girl,"
he says.
"Ah no," Mam whispers.
"She's more than that.
Much more."

Da tries to smile.
"True," he says.
"She has a lot to say."
Mam takes a breath,

struggles for another.
"Nuala will always need help,"
she says.

I see Nuala's beautiful face,
her light hair,
her uneven teeth.
My little sister is slow to speak,
slow to understand.
"I count on you, Anna."
Mam tries to grip my hand.
"Read," she says.
"I'm sorry there was no time for school."

Hours later,
she's gone.
There's only the sound of crying
in our house.

Saying Goodbye

MAE Donnelly comes
to help.
She opens the window.
"To let her spirit
roam free," she says.

Da stands outside
with the men.
The women bring food,
along with memories
and stories,
and even laughter.

Liam stands with me.
He touches my cheek
and shoulder.
I lean against him.

Later, we keen,
Jane and I,
and the Donnellys,
the sound of our crying
spilling out across the field.

We listen for the *beansidhe*,
one of those creatures
who wail when someone dies.
But it's silent
except for the sound
of the night insects.

People from town
I hardly know
come to the church
for Mam's Mass.
I sit between Jane
and Nuala,
holding their hands.
Father Tom tells us
Mam was a good woman.
He calls her Margaret.
I close my eyes.

Dad always called her Maggie,
and sometimes, My Pet.

Our eyes are dry.
No tears are left.

The Well

MAM'S apron
hangs on a hook.
The sash is torn,
I tear off the edge.

Nuala comes with me
to Patrick's Well.
Pieces of fabric crowd
the tree branches overhead:
faded collars, ragged hems,
a bit of blanket.
"Prayers," I tell Nuala.
"Begging for health,
for a fine crop.
Everyone needs something."

I reach up
and add Mam's sash.
"Mam wants?" Nuala asks.

"I want," I tell her.

"Peace for Mam."

I hesitate.

"And to keep my promise

to her."

A shrine with a holy well and a tree full of scraps of fabric left by pilgrims in Ragwell Glen, Clonmel, County Tipperary

(This image is reproduced courtesy of the National Library of Ireland L_ROY_08496.)

St. Mary's

WE stumble through spring.
I dress Nuala,
pull burrs out of her hair.
I try to be Mam.
But the soup I cook is watery,
the porridge thin.

Ah, but the bread.
Mine is exactly like Mam's.
I remember:
the oats,
the fermented potato yeast,
scraping sugar
from the tin,
adding water.

The first time,
I saw my bread rise,

I threw my arms around
Mam's waist,
smiling,
so proud.
And Mam said,
"Teaching you how to do it
was the best part,
passing it on.
You'll always have it now."

One afternoon,
I walk to St. Mary's,
where Mam rests under the sod.
She's not alone.
Baby Aiden lies in a box
next to her,
my tiny brother
who never opened his eyes.
He'd be older than Nuala now,
younger than Jane.
Mam and Aiden together.
Maybe they comfort
each other.

"I'm trying,"
I whisper to Mam.

Her voice comes back to me.
"Read. Read."

The Rent

DA hears about a tax
on glass.
That night,
we board up our one window
with splintery pieces of wood.

In the morning,
the Englishman's agent pounds
on our door.
He's an ugly man,
with blue eyes that bulge.
His voice is sharp.
It's not like our soft Irish.

"The rent will be raised this quarter,"
he says.
Da points to the boarded window.
The man shrugs.
We could have saved ourselves
the trouble,

our bruised fingers.
"Not fair," I yell.
The agent frowns,
and Da shakes his head at me.

The English want us out,
their sheep to graze on our land,
or strangers to pay higher rent
for houses built by Irish hands.

Later, we pry the wood
from the window.
Torn nails,
but it's lighter inside.

We don't talk about the new rent.
But we know we can't pay,
unless the weather is fine
and the crop is huge enough
to sell most of it.

Above me, a streak of lightning.
I climb my hill
to quiet the fear in my chest,
and look down at our house.
The walls need a whitewash,

but if the house looks cared for,
there will be more tax.

Wait.
Is that Nuala I see?
She's opening the half door
to go outside.
Where is Jane
who should be watching her?

"Go back," I call.
Nuala can't hear me.
She dances around
on feet that fit in the palm
of my hand.
She wants to chase the hens
and gather up the feathers.

Jane leans against the door now,
curling her hair in her fingers.
She's dreaming of our brothers,
dreaming of America.

She grows thinner every day,
as Mam did.
Her face is the color of milk.

Her hand that sliced the potato
never really healed.

If only I could give her
more food.
If only I could give her
that dream.
But she'll never sail away
on a ship
that costs more than we have.

I hurry down the hill,
to scoop Nuala up.
I take a feather out of her mouth,
and tuck it between her fingers.

Another Promise

LIAM comes down the road,
pushing a cart
that holds their few things.
His mam walks beside him,
her shawl pulled over her head
in shame.

Liam stops when he sees me,
but his mam walks on slowly.
"We're for the road,"
he says.
"Someone will have our house."
His voice is bitter.

Nuala knows something is wrong.
She hugs Liam's legs.
"Ah, ah," she whispers.

"Where will you go?"
I ask.
He shakes his head.
"A long way from here,
to Cork in the south."

He reaches for the cart handle,
but he turns back.
"One word isn't enough, Anna.
Remember the schoolmaster.
Ask him to help you read.
He's a good man.
He won't say no."
"Maybe," I say,
remembering Mam's voice.

He takes both my hands
in his.
But not to swing me
as he usually does.
He holds them tight.
"I'm coming back, Anna.
Look for me."

"I will," I say,
and call after him.
"Don't forget me."

"Never,"
he calls back.

Oh, Liam.

An evicted family in County Donegal in Western Ireland

(This image is reproduced courtesy of the National Library of Ireland L_IMP_1507.)

Reading

HOW can I ask the schoolmaster,
a girl like me,
who never had time for school,
who writes her name with an X?

But Liam is right.
One word isn't enough.
I'm desperate
to know all of them.

I'm afraid of the schoolmaster,
even though he knows my name,
and nods
when we pass in the village.

But Da says,
"I wanted school
for all of you."
He raises his shoulders,
spreads his hands.

"But the fields," he says.

"The planting.

The house."

He takes a breath.

"Why not at the end of the day?"

"Why not?" Nuala echoes.

I might.

The Schoolmaster

IT'S late.
Still he's outside the school,
staring up at the gray sky.
My throat is closed,
my teeth hidden behind my lips.
But at last, I begin.
"I found a book on the hill."
I hold it out.
"Horse," I say,
pointing to the picture.

He nods,
this white-haired man,
whose head is filled with knowing.
He takes me inside
to a room with a banked fire
in the hearth.
Books line a shelf.
I take a quick look

behind the fall of my hair.
Ten books?
Twelve?

I drop my glance
to the floor.
"Sit," the schoolmaster says,
but I shake my head.

He dips a writing tool
into a pot of black dye,
and writes letters inside the book.
"Anna Mallon," he says.
"Your name."

He spells out the letters,
his fingers running along
underneath.
I stare at them.
A, a mountain, begins my name.
M, two mountain peaks, begins Mallon.
I won't forget.

The National School, Drumlish, Co. Longford, Ireland
(This image is reproduced courtesy of the Historical Picture Archive.)

Hungry July

THERE'S not much to eat:
handfuls of oats for bread,
cabbage, the outer edges dark.
The potato bin is less than half full.
There's so little to get us
to the next harvest.

Our hens are slow
to lay eggs.
I count on one for Da.
He needs strength
to work in the field.
And Jane, so pale,
must have one too.

But Nuala cries for food,
her fingers in her mouth.

"Alannah, my Anna," Da says.
I know what he's thinking.

I spring up from the table,
and step over one of the hens.
We leave Nuala with Jane,
our dreamer.

Da and I steal through the trees,
around the bramble bushes,
as quiet as whispers,
and pry open the iron gate.

We hear the trickle of water
before we reach the stream.
This ribbon of river,
teeming with fish, was ours,
the Mallons',
before the English came.
They own it all now:
the road, the house,
the soil itself.

We hurry through the land
they think is theirs,
and crouch at the river's edge.

How clear the water is.
Pale sand and stones gleam
underneath.

Da makes small waves
with his cupped hands,
as I hold out my apron.
A fish swims in,
and then another.
Caught!

Da squeezes my shoulders.
"Supper," he breathes.
We're happy with our work.
The fish will make a fine meal,
crisped and surrounded
by greens and white mushrooms
from the side of the boreen.

If only Mam were here to share it.
My throat burns.
She taught me
which mushrooms to gather,
which of the wild greens.

If only I could see her
for just one day,
even for a moment.

Da and I hurry away.
We can't take chances.
How terrible to be caught
like a pair of fish.
What would happen to us then?

Shapes

MOST late afternoons,
I study letters
with the schoolmaster.
Once, on the way,
I pass Mae
digging in her field.
She smiles at me.
"Reading again?"
I nod.
"So lucky," she says.
I wave and keep going.
I know I'm lucky.

I can say the letters
as quickly as coins spilling out
of a jar.

The schoolmaster is patient,
friendly.
Why was I ever afraid of him?

I tell him my thoughts
about letters.
"The *h* is like a rush chair,"
I say.
"The *o* is a potato.
The *r* is a shepherd's hook,
the *s*, a fish."

The schoolmaster says it's good
to imagine.
It's what writers do.
"Right here in Longford,"
he says,
"A woman wrote a book
about poor farmers.
And in Dublin,
A man wrote about a giant."
Imagine that.

Rain

I climb my hill,
head down against
the spitting drops.
I pray for sun,
or even a cloudy day.

If the rain doesn't give over,
the land will be soaked
and the crop ruined.
No lumpers to eat.
No vegetables to sell.
How will we pay the rent?
Please...

I look toward Liam's,
the empty house,
the bare field.
I try to swallow the ache
in my throat.

That night,
Da takes the pitcher
from the shelf.
He spreads the few coins
on the table.
He counts, whispers:
"Not enough.
Not nearly enough."

We're not all right.
But didn't we know that
all along?

Da's face is like granite,
his mouth grim.
I see his fear.
I feel it too.

Da was just a boy in 'forty-seven,
when the potato plants oozed black.
People tottered down the road,
carrying their babies,
their mouths stained green
from eating grass.

And last year, almost as bad.
Will we be for the road?

"The crop will hold,"
I manage,
and reach for Da's hand.

He sighs. "Ah, Anna.
You're the heart of this family."
Nuala looks up at me.
"Heart," she says.
Jane nods, smiling.

A family in front of their home near Clonbrock House Estate, Ahascragh, eastern County Galway

(This image is reproduced courtesy of the National Library of Ireland CLON618.)

Awake

I don't believe
the rain will stop,
or the crop will grow.

I sit at the hearth
and say letter sounds
to comfort myself.
MMM.
RRR.
SSS.

The schoolmaster is more patient
than I am.
I want more than shapes,
more than sounds.
I want words!

But he says,
"It will all come,

words, sentences,
stories."

When?

Then on this night,
with rain
covering the field
with mud,
it happens.
I put letters together
with their sounds.
Da.
Mam.

I reach for my book.
Words jump out at me:
Hay, oat, run.

Can I read?
Maybe.
Yes.

I spring up,
twirl around the chair,
dance in front of the hearth.
Oh, Mam,
I can read.

The Stranger

In the morning, someone walks
around the house.
and peers through the crack
in the door.

He wears a bowler hat
and a black suit tinged green
with age.

I tiptoe to the door and wait.
I don't open it
until his footsteps move away.

He stands at the corner
of our field,
with the potato plants
bent in the rain.
I know what he's doing.
He's imagining

the Englishman will put us out,
and him in.

And something else.
Was he the man who tried
to steal the hens?

"Ours," I yell.
He glances back, tips his hat,
then goes toward the road,
but slowly,
his back telling me it's ours
only if the rain stops.

The Letter

MR. Connell from the post office
trudges up the path.
He brings us an envelope
written over
and marked with colored paper.
It comes all the way
from America.
I see our Mallon name
written on front.

Da opens it carefully.
Dollar bills fan out.
Enough to pay the rent!
Mr. Connell smiles.
Da and I hold hands
with joy.
The house will be ours
for another year,
and maybe longer.

We lean over the letter.
Someone has printed it
for my brothers.
Words jump out at me:
work, bridge, Brooklyn.
I run my fingers
over the page.
"Jane can come," I read aloud.

She scoops up the letter,
holds it to her face.
"America," she breathes.
"At last."

Da and I stare at each other.
I bite my lip.
I want to cry, to scream.
The money that would have saved us
will pay for Jane's passage.

Da pats my hand,
trying to make me feel better.
We both know Jane needs to leave.
In America, she has a chance
to eat, to heal,

to live.
We can't say no to that.

At last she takes the road
my brothers have taken,
traveling with a woman
from the town.
We wave goodbye,
Nuala's small arms out.
"Come back, Jane,"
she cries.

In our house,
I close my eyes,
only three of us are left.

The Little People

I learn about the horse
from my book:
where he grazes,
what he eats,
how fast he runs.

"It's all true,
not a made-up story,"
the schoolmaster says,
"We call that nonfiction."

My life,
as well as the horse's,
is nonfiction.

We turn to the horse's last page.
"It's time for another book,"
the schoolmaster says.
"I will lend you mine."
He hesitates.

"The old potato you carry,"
he begins.

"It's for the little people,"
I say.
"I'll throw it
and run
while they eat."

He reaches for a book
on the shelf.
Fairy Tales.
He leans forward.
"They're not real,
fairies and elves,
and little people."

I shiver,
glance at the door.
No one is there.
Could the schoolmaster
be right?

I stay up reading,
most of the night.
I finish the book.

All of it.
Something else about
books.
They teach:
Fairy tales and little people
aren't real.

I wish I could tell you,
Liam.

Fall

AT night,
rain thrums against the earth.
During the day,
mud oozes up between our toes.

Da and I harvest the poor crop.
Nuala toddles back and forth,
her hands full of wet soil
and a small misshapen lumper.
"I eat, Anna?" she asks.
My voice is choked.
"I'll cook it for you."

Da looks across the wheelbarrow
at me.
This small crop won't get us through
the winter.

And winter is coming.
I see it in the gray sky

with its ragged clouds.
I feel it in the air,
smell the cold.

Days later,
huge snowflakes fall,
like the feathers Mam used
to stuff our pillows.
I feel her warm hands on mine,
as I helped fill them too.

Nuala loves the white
that covers the field.
She takes my hand.
"Out, Anna," she says.
"Now!"

We fly outside,
hands up to catch the flakes,
our feet bare and freezing.

I see our few chickens,
still, unmoving,
mounded under the snow.
My hand goes to my mouth.
Nuala reaches for one.

"No!" I say.
"Chickens sleep," Nuala says.
I nod.

Gone from cholera!
The eggs!
The food!

I sink down
on the wet, snowy ground.
It's too much.
What can I do?
How will I keep going?
I'm a Mallon.
But Da is right.
I'm only a slip of a girl.
How can I help us survive?

Nuala watches me,
mouth open,
crying.
I drag myself up,
Somehow,
I have to go on.

The River

Da has gone to the village.
Nuala and I are alone.
She cries with hunger.
What would Mam do?
What can I do?

I listen to Nuala's sobbing.
"We'll catch fish," I tell her,
and wrap her small feet
in old cloths.
"We'll be quiet as mice
inside a barn."

At the river,
a skim of ice covers the water.
I raise a rock
and throw it hard.
Droplets splash up,
as cold as the ice.

I step in,
numbing my feet.
I raise my apron,
a bowl for the fish
to swim in.

Nuala circles a tree.
She stops,
stares over her shoulder.
Is someone coming?
Birds startle up.
I hear footsteps.

I splash out of the water,
grab Nuala's hand
and run.
The footsteps come after us.

Nuala is slow, too slow.
I swing her up,
over my shoulder
and dash through bushes,
over stones,
heart pounding

as we reach the lane.
But we're not safe yet.

I skitter inside our house.
shut the door!
Lean against it!

I peer through the crack
at the Englishman's agent.
He stands in the boreen,
staring about
with his bulging eyes,
not sure of who we are,
or where we went.
He turns back.

I sink down on the floor,
shivering,
with Nuala still in my arms.
She runs her hands
over my hair.
"Ah, Anna, ah," she says.
"No fish."

Liam's House

FROM my hill,
I see a curl of smoke
from Liam's chimney.
The man with the bowler hat,
stands in the doorway.

My hand covers my mouth.
Liam's hearth!
The rooms above
and below!
I'm filled with anger.

Later, when I pass the house,
the man waves.
I turn my back.
Let him see that anger.

Counting

I treat the lumpers like babies,
watching over them.
Da needs five every day,
Nuala one or two.
I try to make do
with three.

Not enough.
Not nearly enough.
The oats are gone.
And now the fish are lost
to us.

I read the schoolmaster's books,
one after another.
They make me forget
the hole in my stomach.

But then,
someone bangs at the door:
the agent,
He wants the rent this week.
The earl's sheep are waiting
for us to leave.

Sheep grazing on the Clonbrock House Estate, Ahascragh, eastern County Galway
(This image is reproduced courtesy of the National Library of Ireland CLON1646.)

The Big House

ONCE I saw the earl,
sitting high on his gray horse,
an ordinary man,
shorter than Da,
with small hands and feet.
Yes, ordinary.
Suppose I went to him,
and begged for more time?

I'm afraid,
but it's what I have to do.

I wait for Da to go to town,
then rush Nuala
down the boreen.
"Please," I ask Mae,
"will you keep her
for an hour or so?"
She nods
and hugs Nuala to her.

Back at our house,
I shake out my skirt
and comb my hair with my fingers.
Wearing Willie's torn jacket
and John's stiff shoes,
I take the road to the big house
and push open
the great iron gates.

I know I can't knock
on the massive doors.
I go around to the back,
and even there,
the door is twice as wide
as ours.
I take a breath, and rap,
head down against the biting cold.

The cook peers out at me,
I know her from the village.
She must eat three pounds of potatoes
a day.
Mae Donnelly said once,
"That plump soul is sweet on the agent."

The cook laughs when I say,
"I want to see the master,"
and turns me away from the step.
"Wait," I say.
Too loud.
I say it again,
softer.
Better?

She doesn't answer.
I listen to the clatter of plates,
the smell of roasting lamb.
Anger fills my chest.
"Mallon land," I yell.

A girl sits at a window.
She glances at me,
as if I'm an insect
that crawls along the path.
What does she care
if we lose our house,
our land?

I pick up a rock,
raise my arm.

A manor house in Edgeworthstown, County Longford
(This image is reproduced courtesy of the National Library of Ireland L_CAB_09217.)

I'll hit the side of her house.
Let her see I'm not an insect.

I aim.
Throw.
Glass shatters.

I run.

Waiting...

THE cook knows who I am.
Wouldn't she guess
I'd broken the window?
Wouldn't she tell?
Will I be taken away
from Da and Nuala?

I watch the the boreen,
stay close to the house.

A day passes,
then a second.
I've read three
of the schoolmaster's books.
But my horse book is still
my favorite.

I turn the pages,
look toward the boreen.
No one comes.
Am I all right?

The Agent

I stir up the fire
on this cold morning,
the start of winter,
and wrap Mam's wool shawl
around Nuala.

Da is outside.
Nuala stares up at me
with her huge gray eyes.
"He yells. Not happy?"

I open the half door,
to see...
Da waving his arms
at the English agent
and his men.

My heart almost stops.
I hear him say *window*.
I hear him say *glass*.

Nuala darts outside,
shawl dragging.
"Go," she says,
waving them away.

One of the men tosses her aside,
as if she's a hen or a cat.
It's too much for me,
too much for Da.
We throw ourselves at the men,
hitting, shoving.
I yell, using words
I've never said before.

They drag us down,
and push our faces into the mud.
We're trussed up
like spring lambs,
and shoved into their cart.
The horse clops away from Nuala.
Her arms reach for us.
"Anna," she cries.
Oh, Nuala!

The Barracks

WE pass Liam's house.
The man stands outside,
staring at us.

Mae stands at her door,
as we pass the Donnellys'.
Blood is smeared across
my cracked teeth.
My lips are thick.
Still I try to scream,
"Nuala, left alone!"
Does she hear me?

The cart turns.
We're on our way to prison.
Inside,
they pull off our ties.
They won't let me sit near Da.
I'm forced against a damp wall
that drips with water.

Only a few sods of peat
warm this fortress.
I rub my icy feet together.
The wind sweeps in,
and waves papers on the desk.

A constable points his finger
at me.
"You tried to injure the earl's men.
That's a crime."

He frowns.
"And worse,
you broke the window,
slicing the daughter's sleeve.
Did you think
with that red hair,
you'd get away with it?"

I look around.
I have to escape.
The barracks door isn't closed
all the way!
I see a wedge of gray sky,
a sliver of road.

I throw myself to my feet,
and slide through the space.
I circle the horse and cart
in front,
and dive across the road.
I don't look back.

The field is circled by rocks,
by trees.
I scramble into them,
and crouch behind rough boulders.

The door bursts open all the way.
The men shout;
their feet pound across the road,
into the narrow field.

Will they see me,
almost buried
in these rocks?
My arms cover my head,
hiding my give-away hair.
I'm a kneeling statue,
except for the trembling,

and the breaths
I must take.

I could reach out and touch
their muddy boots.
They're that close.
"She can't go far,"
one of them says.
They move away,
still searching.

I wait for a long time,
until I'm soaked from the snow
beneath me.
I try to move,
but feeling is gone.
I rub my hands against my chest,
until they burn,
and then the soles of my feet.

The constable is wrong.
I can go far.

The Longford Road in Drumlish, County Longford
(This image is reproduced courtesy of the Historical Picture Archive.)

❧ Away ❧

Escape

HOLDING my skirt
above my ankles,
I tear through the cemetery
and splash along the creek.

I cross the road,
peering over my shoulder.
I don't see them.
Not yet.

I trip
and go down hard,
my hands scraped,
a great tear in my skirt.

If only I could sleep
on this snowy ground,
for a moment.
But I scramble up.
Hurry, Anna, run.
I tell myself.

I reach our house, still there,
but inside,
everything is turned over
or broken.

"Nuala," I call.
She doesn't answer.
Could she be at the Donnellys'?
Please be safe, little sister.

A cup is shattered.
Mam's favorite.
She'd hold it to her lips,
then reach out
to share a sip of tea.

I bend,
touch a shard.
The rush chair is on its side.
Oh, my book is underneath.
I reach for it
and tuck it in my skirt.
Safe.

At the doorway,
I stop for a last look.

Will I ever see my house again?
Or will the English tumble it
to the ground,
roof thatch scattered;
our bits and pieces,
an apron, a bit of a comb,
blown in the wind?

I almost see Mam,
lying on the bed.
I almost hear my voice,
the promise I made
to take care of the house,
the land!
Will I ever keep my word?

I run along the boreen
to the Donnellys' place.
Their chickens startle up
with a flurry of feathers,
as I dart around them.

"Nuala, are you there?"
I call, my voice ragged.
Mrs. Donnelly comes to her half door,

swings it open.
"She's here, child, don't worry."

I rush past her.
I have only seconds.
Mae puts Nuala in my arms,
a tornado:
hands waving, legs kicking.
"Put me down."
"Ah, Noo-la," I whisper,
stretching her name.
"Ah, my girl."

I don't stop.
One hand brushes
Mae's shoulder.
I nod at Mrs. Donnelly,
small thanks
for taking care her.

Outside, I'm away from all I love.
I'm wanted.
On the run.

And Da!
Cold and hungry,
caught in the barracks.

Holding Nuala,
I try to think:
Where can we go?
There's an aunt
I've never seen,
a Rogers like Mam.

"Ethna's a weaver,"
Da said.
Stern and unfriendly,
she lives near the shore
of Lough Ree, outside Athlone.
Will she help us?

The sky fills with sleet.
Nuala sleeps, her face damp
against my neck.
My arms ache.
I slip and slide in the mud.

It's still light,
but night is coming.

Three girls in an old stone ruin near Clonbrock House Estate, Ahascragh, eastern County Galway

(This image is reproduced courtesy of the National Library of Ireland CLON2156.)

The Shed

AHEAD of us is a shed.
Its doors bang open and shut.
I dart inside.
If I reach out,
both arms would cover its width.

Are we safe here?

Bales of hay have become undone.
I throw handfuls over us.
Hiding us.
Warming us.

Nuala sleeps.
I stare at the starless sky,
through a hole in the roof,
and watch the moon
riding in and out
of the clouds.

I wonder . . .
will we reach Aunt Ethna?
"She's skinny as a spider,
with a sting to match,"
Da had said.

"She's known for her weaving,"
Mam had added.
"Her work is truly beautiful."
Mam smiled.
"She uses a loom
built by our great-grandfather.
It's a lovely thing,
Unusual."

Da shrugs.
"Amazing that such a woman,
always angry, it seems,
can do what she does."
He smiles too.
"Everyone has something."

I wonder . . .
will I be caught
before I find her?

Dragged back to prison,
for how long?
Forever?

An ache in my chest
comes up to my throat.
Home, I think,
the rush chair,
days when we were all together:
Da, my brothers, and sisters,
Mam teaching me how
to make colcannon,
shredding cabbage,
slicing potatoes,
humming.

On a summer evening,
I chased Liam
across the field's edge,
stopping breathless,
sinking down,
leaning against each other.

The Farmer

THE shed door scrapes open.
I startle up,
covering Nuala with one arm.
An old man with a pitchfork
rears back,
shocked to see two filthy waifs
nestled in the straw,

Nuala wakes and begins to cry.
Can I grab her?
Dart around him?
But the farmer says,
"Now, now."
He rests the pitchfork
against the wall.
"Come up to the house."

Will he turn us in?
My heart pounds.

I hold Nuala on my shoulder.
I can't get around him,
can't get away.
I feel my book at my waist,
as we go inside.

Food

FARM tools are stacked
against the wall.
A scruffy dog lies
under the table.

"Lost your place, did you?"
the farmer says.
He heats porridge over the fire,
and pours it into bowls.
"Sit," he says.

With my sore feet lightly
on the dog's willing back,
I raise the bowl to my mouth
and swallow, swallow.
The warmth spreads
from my throat to my chest.
His porridge tastes like Mam's,
thick, filling.

"The bailiff is coming here,"
he says, and shrugs.
"This morning? Tomorrow?
Then I'll be at my son's,
my house gone."

I hear the words,
Bailiff coming . . .
this morning . . .
I grab Nuala's hand
from around the bowl.
I pull her up,
her chin dripping.
She screams, "Eat."

I pay no attention.
I drag her out of the man's house.
"Ah," he says behind me.
He knows now I'm on the run.
"Hurry," he says.
"Go."

I stand at the step,
And look around wildly.
Nuala's sobs against my ear.

Which way?

South. I want to go South.

But there's no sun to guide me.

I must have spoken aloud.

He points.

"That way."

Yes.

I run.

Stumble.

Nuala screaming again.

I kiss her filthy face.

Then, limping,

I go on.

The Road

I stop at last,
and hide behind a hedgerow.
Are we far enough away?
Can Nuala still be heard?
I put my hand gently,
over her open mouth.
"We are mice," I whisper.
"Remember?"
She nods uncertainly.

"No one can hear us."
I wipe her face with my skirt.
I'm up again,
Nuala at my side now.
We cross a field
puddled with snowmelt,
the first of many.

How far is it to find the Aunt,
with her spider sting?

How far is it before we see
Lough Ree?

Nuala tires
after chasing a rabbit.
She raises her arms to be held.

I see a road ahead.
Should I chance it?
I look back.
It will get us away faster.

I follow the road.
It turns,
and we turn with it.

Nuala points to people
as we pass them by.
One woman pushes a cart.
A child leans over the side,
a baby I can't see is crying.
Another family walks slowly,
the father bent,
carrying a pack.

There are others.
Everyone is searching for a place
to stay,
somewhere safe,
now that the English have taken
their own places.

Will we go home one day,
with Da there,
to fold us in
with loving arms?

Oh Da, where are you?
I need you.
I'm so afraid.

An eviction on the Vadeleur Estate, Kilrush, County Clare

(This image is reproduced courtesy of the National Library of Ireland L_ROY_01767.)

Traveling

THE road takes us to a village
with a blackened stone church,
its steeple caught in the mist.
My arms are numb from holding Nuala.
Maybe we could go inside
and say a *Hail Mary*
while I put Nuala down
next to me.

Two policemen stand
in the road, twirling batons,
watching us.
Can they see that I'm wanted?

I walk past them quickly,
head down,
shoulders hunched,
until we're out of their sight.

But that's not for now.
Now is for Nuala.
Now is for milk.

Back inside,
the Aunt points to a rack
with a few chipped cups.
I take only one and pour.
Cream rises to the top.
I long for a sip.
But, "Both hands, Nuala," I say.
She reaches for it,
still on the Aunt's lap,
and gulps the milk down.
I look away.

The Aunt twitches one bony shoulder.
"Is it a saint you are?"
She glares at the ceiling,
where a cobweb floats gracefully.

I'm no saint.
I pour a scant cup for myself,
and sip it slowly, making it last.
Thank you, saint of the well.

The Aunt points to the room
below the hearth.
"I suppose you could sleep there."
I can hardly keep my eyes open.
I reach for Nuala.

Hair flying,
she shakes her head.
The Aunt almost smiles.
"There's room for the child
in my bed," she says.

I take the empty cups,
wipe them out,
then go into the small room,
to sleep alone,
without a sister.
I allow myself a few tears.
But the dog climbs up,
and warms my feet.
I whisper his name
gratefully.
"Madra."

Days

THE days pass like beads
on a string.
The first day,
I watch the Aunt milk the cow,
with Nuala leaning over her.
Milk spurts into the pail.
"I'll do this from now on,"
I say.

She doesn't answer.

The second day,
she brings six chicks inside.
"I'll feed them from now on,"
I say.
She puts a chick in Nuala's hands
and looks away from me.

Every day I sweep.
Please see that I'm a worker.

I know she notices.
Nothing escapes her,
except the sound of words,
the clucking of hens,
the moo of the cow,
the bark of the dog.
My voice.

She doesn't have much to eat.
But she shares what she has,
without a word.

One morning, I walk around
to the shed . . .
and jump!
A boy.
I've seen him before
in the next field,
tending to his sheep.
He has the beginning
of a messy beard.
His sleeves are ripped.
Strings hang from his jacket,
where buttons used to live.

What is she talking about?
For Nuala's sake,
I don't say a word.
Then I see.
The edges are a mess.

She shows me how to pull them
even.
"Better, yes?" she says.

I find the rhythm
after a while.
It's not so different from reading.
Can't miss a stitch.
Can't miss a word.

I turn to the Aunt.
I catch her nodding.
I smile,
and she gives me an almost smile
back.

A loom inside a cottage in Donegal, County Galway

(This image is reproduced courtesy of the National Library of Ireland L_ROY_09179.)

Another Shed

THAT night,
I look for a place
to pile hay over us,
to soothe my blistered feet.
If only Nuala would stop whispering,
"Home, Anna,"
around the thumb in her mouth.

A barn looms up ahead of us.
The house is just beyond it.
No one is outside to ask for food.
To beg!
Da would be so ashamed.

We'll sleep in that barn,
and try not to think
about the holes
in our stomachs,
the cuts on my feet.

With one hand,
I pull open the door.
Inside, there's no wheat,
no grain.
It's empty,
except for a few bits of straw
on the clay floor.

I close us in,
away from the bitter cold,
and wrap Nuala in my arms,
still crying.
We lean against the wall.
Not welcome,
I feel that.

I rest only for a moment.
The door opens.
A woman stands there,
hair and skirt blowing.
I think of her kitchen,
of milk for Nuala,
and maybe an egg for me.

She doesn't say a word,
But with a hoe,
she motions for us to leave.

I pick Nuala up,
asleep now,
edge my way past the woman,
and look for the curve
in the road.

A misty moon lights the fields
and another house ahead of us.
I'm desperate for food,
for sleep.

I knock on the door,
but no one answers.
Is the house empty?

I sink down against the door,
with Nuala wedged in between,
and stare up at stars
burning in the sky.

Do I dare sleep?
Suppose the constable comes by.

He'll see us,
of course he will.
But my eyes won't stay open.

They close until
an owl hoots nearby.
I jump.
My heart pounds.
I sleep at last,
dreaming of Liam.

How Far?

I don't wake Nuala yet.
The sun comes up
and touches us.
It's almost warm
on that damp stone step.

I crouch there, guessing.
How many townlands
still to pass
before we see the waters
of the *lough*?
Before we see the Aunt?

No matter how mean she is,
she'll know we're kin,
and maybe take us in.

I wake Nuala.
It's time to be away

from this empty house,
which looks lonely
in the daylight.

We need food
to keep us going.
Feed the fire,
Da would say,
before it goes out.
And us with it.

We walk through a village,
pass the church,
and a few houses nestled together.
I peer in the small window
of a grocery store
and go inside.
The shelves seem as empty
as last night's house.

A man wearing a shapeless hat
stands behind the counter,
"Please," I begin.
I don't have time for more.

He waves his arms at us.

"Tinkers," he yells.

"Out of here."

I want to tell him

we're not those people

who wander around the country,

strange and different,

begging,

and maybe stealing.

A terrible thought:

Will we come to that?

A woman comes from a curtain

in back.

"Tom," she says, and no more.

She pours us milk from a jug.

She presses brack, still warm,

in our hands.

We sit outside

to eat the fruited bread,

and drink milk

that belonged to a cow

an hour or so ago.

Inside again,
we give back the cups.
The woman is gone.
"Thank you," I say.
The man shakes his head
and turns away.

But I'm strong again.
There's one less village
to go through.

The road circles and winds.
Sometimes I walk on gravel
that's sharp between my toes.
Sometimes I tread along dirt,
with patches of water
that reflect the sky.

My throat is dry.
I reach down,
careful not to jostle Nuala,
and pop a stone into my mouth.
My tongue washes it clean.
I sit on a rocky wall,
and roll it against my teeth.

It's as good as a sip of water.
Almost.

People pass us,
paying no attention,
they have their own troubles
to think about.
A carriage comes by.
I see a woman in a feathered hat.
She has no problems.
She has time to stare at us.
I try not to pay attention.

Instead,
I think about the road
in front of us.

The Well

Lost!
A day wasted,
veering east
instead of south.

Since yesterday,
I've become a thief.
I stole food from a field,
and from a village store.
We're bone thin,
skin bruised,
my toes missing nails.

How many days
have we been on the run
sleeping in sheds,
or on the damp ground?
How long have I carried Nuala,
her arms wound around my neck,

stopping to smooth down her hair,
to tell her I love her?

"Love Anna," she says back.
I count five.
Five days?

This morning,
I see steps going down,
running with water.
Nuala points. "What?"
I shake my head.
"We'll see."

We slide down the stairs,
into a cave.
In the center is a well.
A statue of a woman
leans over it.
A poor statue,
missing hands,
her cloak green with mildew.

"It's a holy well,"
I tell Nuala.

"The statue is a saint,
maybe to watch over us,
but I don't know her name."

Nuala doesn't care about holy wells.
She's thirsty.
We lie on the rocks
and scoop water
into our dry mouths,
bathe our lips with it.

Please, I whisper
to the saint's poor cracked face.
She stares at the water
with painted blue eyes.

I look at Nuala,
the sister I love.
Water drips from her chin.
She should be sitting by the fire
on this cold and miserable day.
She should be in the house
built by Mallon hands
four hundred years ago.

I stand up,
take her hand.
I won't give up,
even if I have to walk
a hundred miles,
a thousand.
I'll get Nuala to a place
that's warm and safe.

I nod at the saint.
"Thank you for the water,"
I say.
Nuala adds,
"Yes."

Outside,
the glistening sun
leads us.
We keep going.

The River

IT's warm today,
and wind pushes us along.
Black-faced sheep with curved horns
chase each other in the field.

Nuala takes her hand away
from mine.
She wants to twirl down the road,
her arms in the air.

The rims of her nails
are crescents of dirt.
Mine are too.
I have to do something
to clean us up.

I pull her along
to the river's edge.
It's wild and deep.

White curls on top
blow in the wind.

We dip our hands and feet
into the swirling water.
"Cold," Nuala says,
splashing herself.

A policeman comes near,
swinging his club.
But we're days from prison,
just two girls taking a rest.
Still I turn my head away,
and feel my heart ticking.

Market day in Athlone, County Westmeath

(This image is reproduced courtesy of the National Library of Ireland L_ROY_02921.)

Lough Ree

CLOUDS are mirrored
on the silver water.
Athlone is down the road,
with houses
sistered together,
split by a gravel road.

I ask about Ethna at a shop.
The man wipes his hands on his apron.
He goes to the door
and points the way.

We're almost there.
The road is hard packed earth.
Sheep graze in a field,
their sides splashed with blue,
their owner's mark.

We come to the Aunt's door
as the sun falls over the land.

Inside, a dog barks
and Nuala hides her face
in my waist.
I want to hide my own face.
Instead, I raise my chin,
shake out my blaze of hair,
and knock on the closed door.

Nothing happens.
No one comes.
I peer through the cracks
at a slice of hearth
with burning peat.
A lighted candle flickers
on a table.

And oh!
The Aunt, wearing a white cap,
sits at a small loom:
the loom Mam's great-grandfather built.
Her back is straight
as a blackthorn tree.

She pays the dog no heed,
so I pound.

My knuckles are raw.
The dog scrabbles at the door
to get out to me.
That brings her to her feet.

I step back
as if I haven't been peering in
at her and her loom.
She opens the door
and eyes me.
"You needn't make that racket,"
she spits out.

If it weren't for Nuala,
I'd go on.
But a surprise.
Nuala, the shy,
the fearful,
holds out her arms.

The old aunt,
spider thin with a sting,
her face lined,
her upper lip like cat's
whiskers,

reaches out and takes her.
She turns back to the loom
with Nuala hanging on.
"Sit, Madra," she tells the dog.

There's nothing I can do,
but follow,
stepping around the dog
who stretches out
on the floor.

The Loom

THE Aunt sits herself
on the rush-seat chair.
With Nuala on her lap,
she runs one hand
over the even lines of wool
on her loom.

"Nuala," I whisper urgently.
Her head turns toward me.
She smiles a crooked smile,
but nestles closer in
the Aunt's arms.

I bite my lip,
take a chunk of my thumbnail.
I can't start feeling sorry
for myself.

The dog watches me,
one ear up,

the other down.
His tail thumps uncertainly,
until I run my hand
over his rough head.
He moves closer
to my feet.
I'm family now.
At least the dog thinks so.

I'm dizzy for food.
I glance at the hearth.
An iron pot swings
to one side.
Is there anything in it?

A quick look at the Aunt's table:
cones of wool lay there,
instead of food.
But maybe the cabinets hold
a jug of oats,
or greens for soup.

"We've come a long way,"
I say,
to remind her of manners.

No matter how poor we were,
we always gave something
to strangers at our door,
if only a cup of water boiled
with a little chickweed.

She pays no attention to me.
Nuala hums one of Da's songs
to herself.

I see Da's face,
those faded blue eyes.
I feel his strength.
I will not ask for food
for myself,
but I have to do it
for Nuala.

"My sister needs..."
I begin.
The Aunt doesn't answer.
I start again.
"She has to have..."

Then I realize:
the dog, Madra,

barked loud enough
to raise the thatch
off the roof.
I pounded at the door
bruising my knuckles.
The Aunt can hardly hear!

I step around in front
of her.
I raise my voice.
"My mother was a Rogers," I say.

She peers at me with old eyes,
milk over blue.
"Do you think I don't know that?"
she says.
"Rogers hair,
red as..."
She doesn't finish.
She begins again.
"My mother, my grandmother.
The color of rusty nails."
She raises her eyes
to the ceiling.

I've often thought it myself.
But, "My father thinks it's lovely,"
I say.
She shakes her head.

"My sister needs something
to drink," I manage,
ignoring my own manners.

"You see I have my arms full.
The child needs care,"
she says as if I don't care
for Nuala.

Miserable old woman!

Nuala pats the Aunt's face.
She pats Nuala's.

"I need to find water for my sister,"
I say.
"In the pot on the hearth,"
she answers.
"But I'd give her milk
from the cow."

A cow!

"Milk cools under the house
in back," she says.
"A rock marks the place."

A Brown Cow

OUTSIDE, I walk around
the house,
weeds high,
my head bent to see
underneath.

In an open shed,
a cow waits patiently
for night to be over.
I pat her broad back,
and step away
from her swishing tail.

Near a pointing rock,
I find the jug of milk,
its metal sides cool.

If we stayed,
Nuala would have milk
every morning,

all from that one cow.
Maybe there'd be hens
who'd lay eggs
for her to eat.
I'd watch her grow strong,
her cheeks growing round,
her arms less like sticks.
If only we could stay
for a while.

I try not to think about my hill,
about my house,
and the hearth.
Is it all still there?
Did the bailiff tumble it
to the ground?
Are our bits and pieces gone?

And Da!
Is he alive somewhere?
I try not to think about Liam.
I'll never see him again.

I touch the book at my waist.
"Horse," I whisper for comfort.

But that's not for now.
Now is for Nuala.
Now is for milk.

Back inside,
the Aunt points to a rack
with a few chipped cups.
I take only one and pour.
Cream rises to the top.
I long for a sip.
But, "Both hands, Nuala," I say.
She reaches for it,
still on the Aunt's lap,
and gulps the milk down.
I look away.

The Aunt twitches one bony shoulder.
"Is it a saint you are?"
She glares at the ceiling,
where a cobweb floats gracefully.

I'm no saint.
I pour a scant cup for myself,
and sip it slowly, making it last.
Thank you, saint of the well.

The Aunt points to the room
below the hearth.
"I suppose you could sleep there."
I can hardly keep my eyes open.
I reach for Nuala.

Hair flying,
she shakes her head.
The Aunt almost smiles.
"There's room for the child
in my bed," she says.

I take the empty cups,
wipe them out,
then go into the small room,
to sleep alone,
without a sister.
I allow myself a few tears.
But the dog climbs up,
and warms my feet.
I whisper his name
gratefully.
"Madra."

He holds a hammer
in one broad hand,
and bangs back boards
that hang loose.
"Martin," he mumbles,
around nails that bristle
in his mouth.
"Anna," I say.

Later, a potato plant pokes
out of the muddy ground.
A miracle:
two praties have grown firm
under the ground.
And we're still here,
Nuala and I.

Spring

Outside,
I squint at the sun
and listen.
Nuala puts her hand
in mine.
"What?" she asks.

It's coming from
Martin's barn:
a sheep bleating.
"Ah," I say. "Spring.
The sheep are being
sheared."

The barn door swings open.
A sheep bursts out.
"No clothes," Nuala says.

I grin and watch,
Martin carries another

He holds a hammer
in one broad hand,
and bangs back boards
that hang loose.
"Martin," he mumbles,
around nails that bristle
in his mouth.
"Anna," I say.

Later, a potato plant pokes
out of the muddy ground.
A miracle:
two praties have grown firm
under the ground.
And we're still here,
Nuala and I.

Spring

OUTSIDE,
I squint at the sun
and listen.
Nuala puts her hand
in mine.
"What?" she asks.

It's coming from
Martin's barn:
a sheep bleating.
"Ah," I say. "Spring.
The sheep are being
sheared."

The barn door swings open.
A sheep bursts out.
"No clothes," Nuala says.

I grin and watch,
Martin carries another

Sheep shearing
(This image is reproduced courtesy of the National Library of Ireland M56/43.)

into the barn.

I agree with Nuala.

Sheared sheep do look strange,

with their winter coats gone.

Wool

THE Aunt glances
toward Martin's barn.
"At least
make yourself useful,"
she tells me.

I hold words back
behind my teeth.
Nuala loves her.

The Aunt flings out one hand.
"Martin needs help."
She pats Nuala's shoulder.
"You can go too, Pet."

For once,
Nuala leaves the Aunt's side
and we cross the field
together.

In the barn,
dust floats in the air.
Filthy swirls of fleece
litter the floor:
the winter coats of his sheep.

Nuala scoops up a wad,
tosses it into the air.
It's oily,
and filled with seed,
brambles, and bits of hay,
I spot a few dried-up bugs.
"Wings gone," Nuala says.
"Can't fly?"

Martin grins at us.
"Before Ethna weaves,
there's a way to go,"
he says.

He shows us
how to run our fingers
through the knots,
pick out the seeds

and twigs,
and dried-up insects.
Poor things.

"Not wool," Nuala says.
"Not yet," Martin agrees.

We spend hours washing
and rinsing over and over.
"And now we card," Martin says,
a word I don't know.
But it makes sense.
We run wire brushes
through the fleece,
then comb it into rolls.

"How did I ever do this alone?"
Martin says,
as he pulls an old blanket
off a spinning wheel
and spins...

Until we see yarn!
"Nice?" Nuala says.
"Perfect," Martin agrees.

I rub my tired back.
But I've made myself useful,
I tell myself grimly,
then grin.

Resting

LATE afternoon.
The cow chews in the field.
The wash dries on the grass.

The Aunt runs her shuttle
through the lines of wool,
and Nuala leans against her knee.

We've been here,
how long?
It's planting time again.
But the Aunt doesn't sow.
Her field grows weeds
and nettles.
"I could start the garden,"
I say,
standing in front of her.

Did she hear?
She pays no attention.
This week, I'll begin anyway.

Late in the day,
I walk to the lough.
Madra, the dog,
comes along.
The sun beams a path
across the water.
I find a place to sit,
and take my book
from my waist.
I know most of it by heart now,
old friends.
I talk the book aloud.

The water ripples.
It reminds me of the stream
at home,
once our very own.
I think of fish
slipping into my apron.
Da smiling.
And, so long ago,
Mam cooking soup
for our supper.

Weaving

THAT night,
the Aunt sits at her loom,
but watches me.
"I will teach you,"
she says.
"You have time on your hands."

She runs her hand
over the smooth wood,
dark with age.
"You won't see a loom like this,"
she says.
"Built by a Rogers
before my time."

I sink down on the floor
in front of the loom.
She puts the small piece of wood
in my hand.
"The shuttle."

She guides my hand.
"No," she says.
She shows me:
in and out.

Sheep's wool,
the color of cream,
runs in even lines
along the loom.
I think of our work,
my back still aching.

"Martin does fine carding," the Aunt says.
"And me," Nuala adds.
"The two of you,"
the Aunt says.
I wind the shuttle through the wool.
I'm learning to keep my mouth
closed over angry words.

The weaving's not hard,
not really.
Only my knees are up,
my feet hard against
the gritty floor.

Nuala watches.
She makes fishlike motions
with her hands.
I do the same,
and the fabric takes shape.

"It grows for the Englishman
in the Big House,"
the Aunt says.

I pull my hands away.
This is for one of them?

The Aunt frowns.
"For now," she says.
"But someday . . ."
Her face is a mass of wrinkles.
"I cannot plow,
but I can do this.
It pays the rent indeed."

She cuts off her words,
scolding.
"Your ends are too wide.
I see loops.
Uneven."

Martin

HE works for the Englishman,
at the Big House too.
"It keeps me here,
my sheep grazing,"
he says in his quiet way.

He puts his own farm to bed
in the dimming light,
then comes to the Aunt's field.

Together,
we plant a vegetable garden.
I picture rows of cabbage,
and potato blossoms
with lumpers hiding underneath.
He sweeps the walk,
repairs the shed door,
and the crumbling rock wall.

We are friends now,
Martin and I.
I help him as much as I can.
Hand him the hammer,
slide the rocks into their places.

"Why do you help Ethna?"
I ask.
I don't say that she's
a miserable old woman.

He grins at me,
knowing what I'm thinking.
"When my mam died,
I was three or four,
alone with Da, a grumpy man,
strict and angry."
He leans against the side
of the house,
and I see something
in his eyes.
The beginning of tears?

"She was there,"
Martin says.

"Hugging me, loving me.
It has been that way,
all these years."

Like Nuala, I think,
like resting her hand
on Madra's head,
like the baby bird
she brought inside yesterday,
feeding it
drop by drop.

Still,
she's a hard woman
to know.

Nuala

I sit on a rickety stool,
and milk the cow.
It's a satisfying sound:
the milk spurting into
the can.
I lean my head against
her warm, broad back.

Nuala comes.
She tugs at my skirt.
I shake my head.
"I have to finish."

She tugs again,
looking toward the house.
She pulls me along:
toward the Aunt
in the room above the hearth.

Still in bed,

her nightcap half covers
her face.
Madra whines on the floor,
nearby.
Nuala sits cross-legged
on the bottom of the bed,
crying.

I touch the Aunt's shoulder,
and pat her cheeks.
They burn with fever.
"Come on, old woman,"
I say.
"Open your eyes.
Nuala needs you.
Nuala loves you."

I put my hand up.
"Wait."
Outside at the pump,
the water splashes
into the bucket.

I run back when it's full
and heavy now,

and set it on the floor
next to the bed.

"Old rags in the kitchen,"
I tell Nuala urgently.
She doesn't understand.
Of course she doesn't.

Back in the kitchen,
I find the rag bag.
I bring back a soft cloth
and swipe it into
the freezing water.

I bend over the bed.
For the next hour,
I dip the cloth
into the water,
and pat her face,
her wrists,
her neck,
then fold it over
her forehead.

I find socks on a chair.
They don't match

in color, or size,
but not important.
I soak them in water
and ease them over
her feet.
Mrs. Donnelly said once,
"It's a way to draw heat
out of the body."

There's nothing more
I know how to do.
Her eyes stay closed,
her breathing loud
in this small, dark room.

Nuala shakes her hands
in front of her own face.
I want to say it will be all right.
But will it?

This is work
for someone who knows more
than I do,
someone who will help
bring her back.
Mam would have known.

But help is far away.
Help is impossible.

And so I begin again,
cooling her fever,
until the bucket water
has lost its own cool.

Nuala sleeps,
worn out from crying,
Madra, the dog, never moves.
He watches the old woman,
his dark eyes troubled.

It's late in the day.
Her eyes flutter open.
She lies still,
as I rub her feet
in socks
that are almost dry now.

She opens her mouth,
but doesn't speak.
She reaches out
slowly,
touches my hand.

Working

THAT night,
I rake the fire
and bury it in peat ash.
In the morning,
the Aunt and Nuala still sleep.
Madra has moved to the doorway.
I begin the day's chores:
the cow to be milked,
and set out to graze.

I shoo the hens
to peck at the grass,
and carry their warm eggs
into the kitchen
in the Aunt's apron.

I feed Nuala a cup of milk,
still warm
from the giving cow,

and an egg boiled
on the hearth.

Then I tiptoe
into the Aunt's room.
She's awake,
her eyes following,
as I sit on the edge
of the bed,
a cup in my hand.

I put my arm
under her head,
to raise her
so she can sip at the milk.
"Easy," I say.
"A little at a time."
She doesn't answer.

I look at her face,
wanting to touch
her forehead,
to see if the fever's
gone.

I don't dare
with her eyes on me.

I work in the kitchen,
washing Nuala's hands,
her feet.
She looks anxiously
at the Aunt's room,
and then at me.
"It's all right,"
I soothe.
"She'll be fine."

Do I tell the truth?

A New Day

A pale sun rises,
rolls over the sky,
toward the mountains
of Mourne.

I have no time
to long for Da
and Liam,
for the sight of my hill.
And oh, my house in Longford,
my own place.

I sweep out the room,
listening to Nuala.
She sings to the Aunt,
an old song,
the words mixed up,
but the sound is true.

I remember my promise
to keep her safe.
But suppose the Aunt doesn't live?
What then?

The Big House

MARTIN stops on his way.
He gives me a small bundle
of chickweed.
"For tea," he says.
I smile. "Yes!"

But I can't help it.
I burst out,
"How can you work
for the Englishman?"

He answers almost fiercely.
"It pays the rent.
You know that."
Then, almost silently,
"And I hear things."

I tilt my head.
What does he mean?
"Change is coming,"

he says.
"People in the west
are banding together
against high rents."

He shrugs.
"They gave me a book,"
he says.
"They're beginning to fear us."
I shake my head.
It's hard to believe.

"They have a hundred books
anyway," he says.
"On shelves in a great room,
near the kitchen."

I think of my one book,
of the schoolmaster's dozen.
I watch after Martin
as he goes down the boreen.

I hear a sound behind me.
It's the Aunt
holding on to the wall.
"The shawl," she says.

"We must finish."
She sinks down on the chair.
"For the rent," she manages.

I work with the shuttle
until she nods: "Enough."
But I don't know how to get the shawl
off the loom.

"I should have taught you,"
she says.
Blaming herself?
She totters to the loom,
loops one stitch over the other.
I see.
I put my hand over hers.
"I can do this."

I take the shawl off the loom.
It's finished,
a gift from Martin's sheep.

It isn't the Aunt's anymore.
It isn't mine.
It belongs at the Big House.

"You'll bring it to the cook
at the back door,"
she says.

"Of course, the back door,"
I answer with bitterness.

"You'll bring it to the cook
at the back door,"
she says.

"Of course, the back door,"
I answer with bitterness.

The Kitchen

I take Nuala's face
in my hands.
"Stay with the Aunt,"
I tell her.
She nods, hesitates.
"I take care of her."
Still at the loom,
the Aunt smiles.
"We'll take care of each other."

I don't bother to see
if the Aunt has shoes.
I'll go to this house
as I am.
Let them see
what they've taken
from us.

Outside,
the gravel is hard

on my soles.
The Englishman's house lies ahead,
almost like the earl's.
Madra follows me.
He stops at the half-open gate.

At the kitchen door,
I knock.
No one answers.
I kick the door open.
There's no one in the kitchen.

I think of Martin's words:
a hundred books.

I fold the shawl
over the back of a chair,
then tiptoe along the hall,
glad my feet are quiet.

An open door.
I look over my shoulder.
No one there.

Inside,
I run my fingers

over the books.
A letter rests
on the table.

I look quickly.
"Charles Parnell in Parliament
tells tenants
to hold back the rent.
Michael Davitt in Mayo
urges them not to pay.
Even in North Longford..."

North Longford?
Us?

I hear voices now.
I can't tell what they're saying.
I frown, thinking.
Do I know one of them?
But I can't be caught.
I rush down the hall,
slide into the kitchen,
without being seen.

The cook runs her hand
over the shawl.

"Ethna did this,"
she says.
"Beautiful, as is all her work."

I nod, thinking of the letter,
trying to place that one voice.
Who is it?

A broadside from 1881 urging tenant farmers to support the Irish National Land League movement

(This image is reproduced courtesy of the National Library of Ireland EPH E124.)

My Book

THE Aunt is at the loom.
Nuala sits on the floor
and plays with the wool.
My chores are finished.
The hens are out back,
the cow in the field.

I talk to my book in my mind.
"Dear book,
we'll go to the lough
and spend time with each other."
And that's what I do.

I throw the Aunt's old shawl,
over my shoulder,
stitches laddered.
It must have been made
before I was born,
but still warm enough
for me to huddle at the lough,

against the wind,
with winter coming.

My hands hold the pages flat.
I read the old friends,
words I know by heart.
I try not to think of home
and Liam
with the few moments I have.

I don't hear the footsteps.
I don't hear the voice
until it's too late.

The Lough

A shadow in front of me,
covers my book.
"I knew I'd find you,"
the voice says.

I look up.
It's the earl's aide.
But why here?
If only Madra were with me.

The aide grabs the book
from my lap,
raises his arm.
Before I can do something,
do anything,
he tosses it into the lough.

I stumble up.
Throw myself into the water.
Feet.

Knees.
Waist.
I try to gather pages
as they float away.

I'm screaming,
wild with grief,
with rage.

I pick up only one page.
The rest are gone.

"Payment," he says,
"for the earl's daughter.
We're even."

I reach out with both arms,
hitting,
punching.
And still he laughs.

"News from home,"
he says.
"Your father is in the house.
And the priest is telling him
not to pay the rent.

They say all of your townland
is up in arms,
up to devilry."

"Good," I yell.
"You'll be gone one day,
and we'll have ours back."

He turns toward the Big House.
He flinches
as I throw a stone.
My aim is poor.
It smashes into the gravel.

Lough Ree, outside of Athlone, County Westmeath

(This image is reproduced courtesy of the National Library of Ireland L_ROY_05267.)

What I'll Do

MY skirt drips water
from the lough.
Absently I bend and squeeze
out the hem.
I'll keep this last page
forever.

I don't have to decide.
I know what I'll do next.
I whisper to Mam,
"Nuala has found a home.
She loves the Aunt.
The Aunt loves her.
I couldn't even take her away."

I go up the road,
and turn off at Martin's house.
He's in front of the shed,
looking surprised to see
the state I'm in.

"Will you . . . ," I begin,
hardly able to talk.
"Anything," he says.

"Take care of the Aunt
and Nuala?
Watch out for the hens
and the cow?"
He nods.
"I'm going to Longford
to take back my house."

"Of course,"
he says.

The Trip

I tell the Aunt,
"I must go home."
And to Nuala,
"I love you."
They both nod and smile.
"Say hello to home,"
Nuala says.

She knows
this is her home now.
She's happy to hold the Aunt's hand,
as I pack up a few pieces of food
to take with me,
and ask if I can take the old shawl.
The Aunt shakes her head.

"Leave it," she says.
She goes to her room.
From under the straw pallet,
she takes a lovely ivory shawl,

its stitches intricate and fine.
She reaches up to wrap it
around me.

"You'll make a fine weaver,"
she says.

I put my arms around her,
Nuala holding us both.
"Dia Duit," the Aunt says.
Go with God.
"I will," I say.
I hold Madra for a moment.
"I love you both," I say,
and realize it's true.

I touch the sodden page
at my waist.
I will keep it always,
and remember
how I learned to read.
I will never forget the aide,
his bulging blue eyes,
his laughter,
his cruelty.

I'll be strong
to get back what belongs
to us,
what has always belonged:
our house,
our land.

Going Home

I leave the house,
the Aunt and Nuala.
From his field,
Martin raises his hand.
I raise mine back.

Out of sight,
I pick up my skirt and run.
Never mind my feet
as they clump onto gravel.
I'm going to see Da.
I'm going to put my arms
around him,
and tell him where I've been.

"Remember the fish in my apron?"
I'll say.
"Remember boarding up the glass
together?"

I pass Athlone.

I know now where I'm going.

The lough is to my left,

and I'll follow the Shannon River above.

I think of home:

the rush chair,

the hearth,

all of us together.

I say their names

as my feet hit the ground:

Mam and John,

Willie and Jane.

Nuala.

Da.

And Liam.

Of course, Liam.

They won't take my house

from me.

The River Shannon, outside of Athlone, County Westmeath
(This image is reproduced courtesy of the National Library of Ireland L_ROY_05256.)

Almost There

I hardly sleep.
I beg a chunk of brack
from a friendly woman.

I run,
walk slower,
stop for only minutes,
bent, my hands on my knees.
I start again.

At last,
I see Liam's house,
the door banging open.
The man in the bowler hat
must be gone.
The man who tried to steal
our hens?

I stumble as I pass
the Donnellys' house.
Almost home.
Almost.

Moments later,
I call:
"It's me, Da.
Anna."

He's out the door,
down the boreen toward me,
tears on his cheeks
that match my own.

Arms out,
we hold each other.
How thin he is.
Is his strength gone?

I hear him whisper,
"Nuala?"
I whisper back,
"Safe."
I smile.

"With the Aunt.
They love each other."

We walk arm in arm,
taking the few steps
across the wide stone
in front.
We cross into the house
I thought I'd never see again.

Da sits in the rush chair,
and I at the hearth,
in the dim light,
smelling the peat
that smolders
in the fireplace.

I warm gruel for us both.
We scoop it up,
feeling its warmth,
tasting its goodness.
Home.

"Now begin," Da says.
And I say the same thing.

Da tells of being left
to walk home.
And I?
From our own long walk,
to safety,
and love.

The Beginning

IN the morning,
a new aide is at our door.
"Tomorrow, Mallon,"
he says.
"You're out of here."

I move in front of Da.
"No."

He looks surprised.
"You'll pay the rent then."
I shake my head.
It's a firm shake,
even though my heart beats
almost loud enough
for him to hear.

"There are sheep to graze,"
he says.
"More grateful than you."

His face is miserable,
his mouth twisted.
"But not more needy."
He glances at the house.

I try to close the door,
but he holds it open
with one hand.

"We'll come with a ramming rod,
and take down the beam.
The house will fall,
raising dust.
You will leave,
never to come back."

Da puts his hand on my arm.
But he can't stop me.
"You cannot make me leave,"
I spit out.

He goes then.
And I sink down at the hearth,
trembling,
fierce,
determined.

A battering ram used during an eviction on the Vandeleur Estate, Kilrush, County Clare
(This image is reproduced courtesy of the National Library of Ireland L_ROY_01772.)

The War

The Priest

FATHER Tom comes late that night
as we hear the church bells chime.
Imagine a priest at our hearth.

"Your name is on the list of evictions,"
he tells us.

Da's face is pale.
His eyes fill
as he looks around our room.
"I know we'll have to leave,"
he says.

"Not this time," I say.
Do I mean it?
How can I stop them?
I think of my promise to Mam.
The house.
The land.
Ours.

The priest clasps his hands.
"Not this time," he echoes.
"Listen to the bells."

The sound is almost joyous,
I think,
as he goes on:
"They'll peal all night
and into the morning
without stopping."

I lean forward.
"People will come from the villages,"
he says,
"from across the fields,
from the farms,
and the townlands.
Our Irish."

Morning

It's just dawn.
The bells still chime.
Above them is the beat
of a drum.

I touch the page of my book
whose words have disappeared
in the lough water.
I hear a thunder of footsteps,
a roar of voices,
coming closer.

I run to open the door.
There's the blacksmith
from Ballinalee,
and McClellan,
the farmer from Drumderrig,
I see the Stakems,
the Donnellys,
and the McNamees.

The schoolmaster raises his hand,
waving to me.

People I've never seen before,
hold sticks or spades.
Some carry pitchforks
over their shoulders.

The boreen is crowded:
women,
men,
girls filling their aprons
with stones from the road.
A grandmother hobbles along
with her cane.
Our house is surrounded,
three deep, four deep.

How can I be afraid?
So many people are here.
Still, I'm afraid.
But I will be part of this.

The bailiff and his men
come from town.
Da and I slip out the door,

to be with the people

who have come to save us.

We are many

against the bailiff's few.

We take our places

in front of the ditch.

I wish I were behind the rocks,

hidden and safe.

But I tell myself we're fighting

not only for my house,

but for all the neighbors.

The bailiff comes toward us,

a big man with a dark beard.

He's stopped before he can get past.

I'm close enough to see

the gray of his eyes.

Is there fear in them?

"We will let you pass,"

Mr. McDonnell says,

"if you don't have eviction papers."

We all know he does,

else why would he be here?

He shakes his head.
"I don't," he quavers.
A girl rushes up to him.
She reaches into his pocket,
pulling out enough paper
to evict four,
maybe five families.

She rips and shreds.
Tosses them into the air.
They scatter like the snowflakes
that have fallen all week.
I catch glimpses of our names
on the torn pieces of paper.

Still the bailiff tries to push
through the crowd.
A stone whizzes past.
It lands inches away from him.

Someone hurls another.
This time it hits his foot.
He jumps back . . .

and retreats with his men,
back the way they've come.

The church bells still peal,
as we sit in the muddy boreen.
For the first time, we've won.
The crowd around me yells,
wild with excitement.

"It's only for now,"
the blacksmith says.
"He'll be here tomorrow,
and more English with him."
He raises his huge arms.
"But we will be here too."

Heat rises in my chest.
I see my book carried
on the waves of the lough,
then sinking
into the moving water,
forever gone to me.
But at last,
I've done something.
I've stood up against those

who'd take everything we love,
everything that's ours,
away from us.

Oh, Liam.
You should be here.

An evicted family outside of their home with their belongings, in Derrybeg, County Donegal.

(This image is reproduced courtesy of the National Library of Ireland L_IMP_1506.)

The Second Day

THIS morning
the crowd is even larger.
People from Cavan,
from Leitrim,
from Roscommon,
take their places with us.

Da reaches for our spades
that are propped against the wall.
"Take one, *alannah*," he says.
I wipe off a clump of soil
and hoist it over my shoulder.

I follow him to the road,
listening to the swell of voices,
the clank of hoes and spades,
heavy footsteps,
the voices of a determined people.

I stand next to Mae Donnelly
as the bailiff comes.

This time he's sure of himself.
I see it in his swagger.
He's surrounded by police,
to protect him, to frighten us.

Someone shouts to us.
Is it Mr. McDonnell?
*"Show your power
and make them feel it!"*

The soldiers try to march
through us.
They point their bayonets.
But we stand firm.

A girl from Ballinamuck
reaches for stones
caught up in her skirt.
She throws one,
and then another.
Both hit the bailiff,
his arm,
his leg.

Now stones come
from all over.

"I am here,"
I shout.
"I'm here for a mam and five girls,
for Liam and his mam,
for me,"
even though he can't hear
with all this noise.

The priest steps in front
of us, arms out.
"Go," he tells the soldiers.
"We don't want bloodshed here
today."

The soldiers and the bailiff
disappear down the boreen,
glad for the safety of their barracks.

I hold the corner of my page
tightly between my fingers.
I'll never let myself be afraid
again.

The Third Day

I couldn't sleep,
but I'm not tired,
not yet.
Hundreds of people will stand
in the snow with us.

Da thinks this will be the
worst day.
We've heard that the English
have sent dragoons
from all over the country.
Dragoons
in their green uniforms!

Da is right.
The force that comes against us
is enormous:
redcoats, dragoons,
local police.

We raise our voices,
throats sore from shouting.
We press forward, slowly,
pushing them back,
showing our power.

And we win.
Win!
They turn,
the mighty English defeated
by a crowd of poor farmers
and a wee slip of a girl
who stood with them.
A girl with only one blue skirt
and wild red hair.
A girl without shoes.

But what she does have
is a shawl given to her
by a woman she's come to love,
and the page of a book
she'll keep forever.

After

The Fourth Day

EVERYONE is gone.
I watched them shoulder
their spades and hoes.
How quiet it is without them.

The priest speaks:
"This is not the end of it.
Prison is ahead
for the leaders.
Rent will still be paid.
Evictions will come.
But it's the beginning.

"What we've done here,
in these three days,
will happen all over
this country of ours."

Yes, the beginning!
I think.
Change is coming.

Some of our men are hauled
to court:
Rogers and McNamee,
McDonnell.
But they return home
soon.

We will still have to pay
rent,
but not quite as high.
The English are wary.
They've managed to unite
a country against them.

But how I will even pay that rent?
Da is stooped now, old.

How?

The Field

As I plant,
a crow swoops down
on a rock.
Its rasping caw is loud
in the silence.

I stand,
rubbing my back.
It will be a small crop,
but the best I can do.

Someone is coming toward
our house,
pushing a cart.
Liam?
Could it be?
But I know Liam's walk.

I frown.
Still this is someone I know.

Could it be the earl's man?
He pauses,
turns into our boreen.

I race home ahead of him.
Inside I lean
against the closed door,
breathless.

"*Alannah?*" Da asks.
I raise my finger
to my lips.

I hear the voice from outside.
"Anna?
Have I come to the
right place?"

I know who it is!
I see his field,
his sheep,
chickweed for our tea.

I throw open the door.
"Martin!"
He sinks down at the hearth,

resting on the warm stone,
and smiling at me.
"Nuala," I breathe.
And Da says her name too.
Martin nods.
"Growing tall.
Taking care of the Aunt."
Da and I look at each other.
The best news!

"I've been sent by Ethna,
with what's in the cart,"
Martin tells us.
"She said you'd know
what to do with it."

Outside,
I climb on the back of the cart.
Lengths of wood newly cut,
smelling sweetly of the tree
it once was.
I open a bag of dowels,
and toss aside a blanket
with cones of wool.
"I will build you a loom,"

Martin says.
"I've studied the Aunt's.
I can do it."

I touch a cone.
"Nuala," he says.
"She prepares the wool,
and weaves beautiful things."
Tears come to my eyes.
If only Mam could know.

"The Aunt told me
it will pay the rent,"
Martin says.
I can almost hear her voice.

Later, I make colcannon:
wrinkled cabbage,
potatoes,
and a little milk Mae
has shared with me,
a meal for the three of us.

My heart is full
for that old woman
who has saved me again.

Mae

MARTIN sands and hammers,
and stands back
to see
how his work is coming.
And I read aloud
from a schoolmaster's book.

Finished one book,
I go for another.

Mae stands outside.
She sees the book
under my arm.
"How lucky to read,"
she says.

"It makes me happy,"
I tell her.

She looks tired today,
worn out.

"If I could read,"
she says,
"it would make me happy too."

I nod and go toward the school,
remembering Mam,
and then her bread.
Why now?
The yeast, the oats,
the wooden bowl and spoon.

I glance back at Mae
working in the field.

"Not the bread,"
I say aloud.
It's Mam's words
I have on my mind.

The best part, she'd said,
teaching you.
Passing it on.

I think of the letters,
the sounds they make,

the words,
the stories.

I could teach Mae
to read!
The best part.
I could pass it on.

Sudden tears:
If only Liam were here.
If he could see me reading,
teaching Mae,
and soon,
weaving.

My Loom

WHEN Martin finishes the loom,
I run my hand over it.
"Like the Aunt's.
Oh, Martin,
I'm grateful."

He brushes the curls of wood
off his shirt and grins.

I pack what food I have
for him to take on the trip
to Athlone.

I stand, waving,
until he's gone.
Then I take one of the cones
and begin my work
to pay the rent.

Hill Street, Drumlish, County Longford

(This image is reproduced courtesy of the Historical Picture Archive.)

Years

A new law has been passed.
We can buy back our houses.
It's a possible amount,
something to work toward.

As always, I climb my hill
in the early evening.
The earl has gone back
to England.
His house is empty
at least for now.

I stop to pick a small primrose,
growing between the rocks
and tuck it in my hair.
I remember finding my book.
I've read the schoolmaster's,
helped Mae with them,
but I've never forgotten
the first.

I look down at our house,
at the road that winds
from the south.
At someone coming.

I feel as if my heart will stop.
But it's only for a moment.
I stumble down the hill,
stones rolling.
I scramble along the boreen.
Calling.
Crying.

Liam holds out his arms,
and I'm inside their warmth.
We rock back and forth.
"I've never forgotten,"
he says.
"Nor I,"
I tell him.

Liam.
Home at last.
Home to me.

Glossary

alannah: Darling child.

astore: My dear.

Athlone: A town on the River Shannon near the south shore of Lough Ree in County Westmeath.

bailiff: A court officer who carries out evictions.

beansidhe (banshee): In Irish mythology a female spirit who wails when someone is dying.

boreen: A narrow country lane.

brack: Bread with fruit, usually raisins.

Cavan: Called the Lake County because of its 365 lakes. It's bordered by six counties, including Longford.

chickweed: A nutritious cool-weather plant with small white flowers that grows at the edge of grass or in fields. It can be eaten raw or cooked. Irish people often used it to flavor tea.

colcannon: A mixture of mashed potatoes and shredded cabbage served hot for dinner. It can be blended with milk and spiced up with a little ham, leeks, or onions.

Davitt, Michael (1846–1906): Founded the Irish National Land League. He wanted Irish land for the Irish people and urged landlords not to charge exorbitant rents.

dragoon: A member of the cavalry in the English army.

Leitrim: A county bordered by Roscommon, Cavan, and Longford counties. It once held five great forests.

lough: Lake.

Lough Ree: A large lake on the River Shannon.

Longford: A county in the Midlands.

Mayo: A county in the west of Ireland where Michael Davitt was born.

Mountains of Mourne: In County Down, the highest mountains in Ireland.

The River Shannon running through Athlone, County Westmeath
(This image is reproduced courtesy of the National Library of Ireland L_ROY_11600)

Parnell, Charles (1846–1891): A member of the British House of Commons and president of the Irish National Land League.

Roscommon: A county bordering Longford, and known for its burial mounds and ancient monuments.

Shannon River: The longest river in Ireland, named for Sionna, a Celtic goddess. It rises in County Cavan, runs through several counties, including Longford, and empties into the Atlantic Ocean.

ramming rod: A large wooden log used to batter down houses when tenants were being evicted.

Author's Note

I remember the first time we went to my beloved Ireland. Jim and I drove from Dublin, stopping at Mullingar for tea, then took the road passing Ballinalee, my heart beginning to race with excitement, looking up at Cairn Hill. Then, at last, Drumlish.

We stopped at a tiny grocery store and I asked about my grandmother, Jennie, wondering about the house where she was born. The grocer pointed. "It's there," he said. "Knock on the door. They'll be glad to see you."

And so we knocked, and I stood where my Irish family lived so long ago. The postmaster's sister made sure I had Father Conefry's book: *A Short History of The Land War in Drumlish in 1881,* a book that told me the house in Derawley, Drumlish, belonged to the Rogers family.

In front of that house, tears streaming, I thought about how my great-grandparents had stood there, lived there, took part in the Drumlish Land War.

Back at home, I read every page of Father Conefry's book more than once. I wanted to write about Ireland, about the Drumlish Land War, about the Rogers house, and the people who were gone before I was born, but who belonged to me.

A Slip of a Girl is fiction, of course. Anna Mallon only loosely resembles my great-grandmother Anna Rogers Mollaghan (Monahan in America.) But the Drumlish Land War really happened, and the house still stands.

We went back many times, Jim and I, and always I put a page of my manuscript under the wishing tree festooned with bits of collars, of aprons, of faded fabric. And my wish? To write truly, to make the people who lived there, who fought for their homes, come alive to those who read my book.

Acknowledgments

I'm more than grateful to everyone at Holiday House, and especially Mary Cash, for her thoughtful editing, which makes such a difference in my writing, and for her friendship, which I treasure; and Terry Borzumato-Greenberg who has also been a dear friend as well as a publicist all these years.

I'm truly indebted to the poet, Sister Immaculata Muldoon, who taught me to love words; to Doctors John Mullee and Arpad Kovacs, who inspired my love of history; and to my mentor, Doctor Sidney Rauch, who believed in me.

A special thanks to Joan Jansen, world's best researcher, and to Rose Kent and Doctor Andrew Duda for all their support.

I so appreciate my family who appear regularly, if anonymously, in my books: Bill and Cathie Giff, Alice and Jim O'Meara, and Laurie Giff; and my grandchildren, Jimmy, Chrissy, Bill and Sarah, Caitie and Stephen, Conor, Patti, Jilli, Haylee, and Aubree.